$ONGO

SONGO
SONGO
SONGO
SONGO
SONGO
SONGO
SONGO
SONGO
SONGO

Songo

(For Children & Families)

Rachel Pantin & Mauricio Venegas-Astorga

Songo (For Children & Families)
First edition published 2018
By Victorina Press
Adderley Lodge Farm
Adderley Road
Market Drayton, TF9 3ST, England.

Music (lyrics, music score & audio) © 2018 West One Music Limited
℗ 2018 West One Music Limited
Project Directors: Rachel Pantin & Mauricio Venegas-Astorga Speech and Language Specialist: Helen Ayres
Music: composed, arranged and recorded by Mauricio Venegas-Astorga & Rachel Pantin
Original idea, concept and original drawing of the character Songo devised and created by Musiko Musika Materi-
als: devised and developed by Musiko Musika Registered Charity no. 1099508
Cover, graphic design and illustrations: Fiona Zechmeister

British Library Cataloguing in Publication Data
A catalogue record for this book is available from the British Library

ISBN: 978-1-9996195-2-7 (Songo For Children & Families)
ISBN: 978-1-9996195-3-4 (Songo For Children, Early Years Settings & Practitioners)

Printed and bound in Great Britain by MTS Duplication 12 Ruperra Close
Old St. Mellons
Cardiff, CF3 6HX, England

Table of contents

Introduction

Songo is founded on the belief that early intervention in promoting successful language acquisition is essential in enabling children to become fully inclusive participants in society as they grow up. This innovative and unique programme of songs and activities has been designed to enhance and support key areas of early linguistic development, in tandem with other early developmental areas that are crucial to successful social, emotional and educational progression. Music provides a wonderful context for this learning because of the way in which it embraces us as a whole person, in rhythm and melody, communication, interaction and enjoyment.

Each song has ideas of activities that you can explore with your child as you become familiar with the songs, providing inspiration for you to engage in a musical and linguistic journey with your child and Songo.

About Musiko Musika

Musiko Musika was founded in 1998 by the musicians and educators Mauricio Venegas-Astorga and Rachel Pantin, with a mission to use world music as a tool to improve the access of children and young people to creative music making, and to support individuals and communities in valuing and sharing their cultural identity and heritage through music. We develop and deliver innovative projects and use our unique expertise to empower socially and economically disadvantaged children and young people and their communities.

Our vision is that the wonderful and remarkable diversity of the world's cultures available in London, England and the world is creatively thriving and celebrated, and is valued and accessible to all as performers, creators, learners and audiences.

Keep in touch and visit the website to access more resources and videos: www.musikomusika.org (Registered Charity no. 1099508)

Songo, Songo

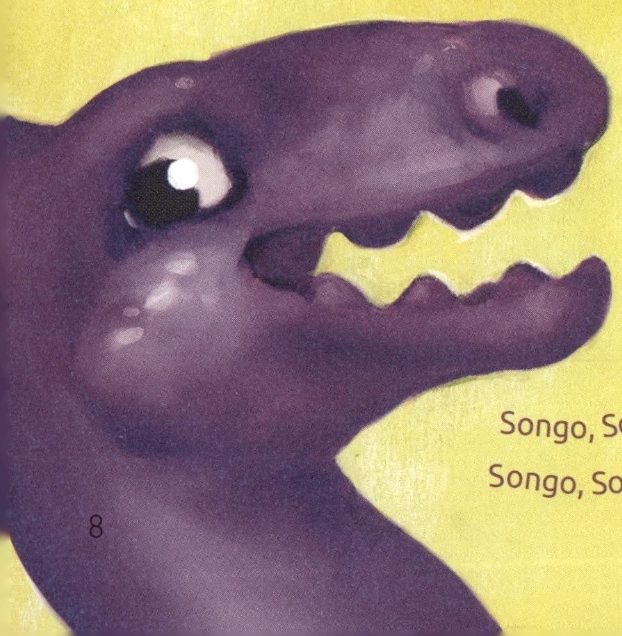

Words for stories, words to share
Words to help and show we care

Speaking, listening, we'll get along
Helping us to learn by singing a song

Songo loves singing.
His favourite song is
Twinkle Twinkle Little Star

Can you sing
Twinkle Twinkle
for Songo, or
share a new song
with him?

Hello

Hello, hello
How many ways are there
to say hello?

Can you sing hello in
a different language?
How about
'Hola', 'Bonjour'
or 'Salam'?

Smile and wave as
you sing the song and
try singing it softly as
well as loudly.

10

Hello, hello
I'm pleased to see
you my friend
Ni hao
Salam
Bonjour
11

Hi There

Shall we sing our
names or how about
'Songo Songo,
that's your name'?

Hi there, hi there, what's your name?
Hi there, hi there, what's your name?
We can sing and dance together
We can play with all our friends

Singing a short solo like this is great for building your child's confidence with their voice.

First Thing in the Morning

First thing in the morning, what do you do?
Jump, jump, jump, jump out of bed

Next you're in the bathroom, what do you do?
Wash, wash, wash, wash your face

Then go to the kitchen,
what do you do?

14

After you have eaten, what do you do?

Brush, brush, brush,
brush your teeth

Finally you're ready, what do you do?
Walk,
walk,
walk, walk to school

Show me how you...
jump out of bed,
wash your face,
eat your breakfast,
brush your teeth,
walk to school...

15

Heads, Shoulders

Heads, shoulders, knees and toes
Heads, shoulders, knees and toes

Clap your hands 
Clap your hands

Clap your hands with me

Heads, shoulders, knees and toes
Heads, shoulders, knees and toes

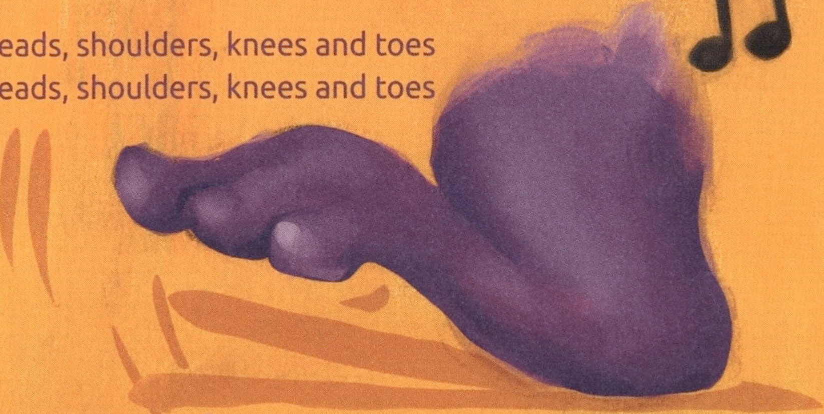

Stamp your feet ✗✗
Stamp your feet ✗✗
Stamp your feet with me ✗✗✗

Put your hands on your head, shoulders, knees, toes...

Moving and using actions help improve coordination,
listening and rhythm skills as well as learning the
names of the parts of the body.

Look at the Sky
Look at the Sky
What do you see?
18

Can you make it thunder with your
hands and feet?

What else can we do together to make
the sound of the rain,
the wind or the sun?

The weather today looks sunny to me

How many leaves
are you going to
choose?

2, 5, 10?

There's a Hungry Caterpillar

There's a hungry caterpillar sitting next to me
Munching, crunching, eating his lunch
How many leaves today?

Developing listening skills, this can be a game by taking turns to play, clap and count the leaves.

How hungry
is that caterpillar
today?

Four, four, four, four,
four leaves today
Four, four, four, four, four leaves today

Munching, crunching,
eating his lunch
Four leaves today

21

Who's That Walking?

Who's that walking
down the stairs

Who's that walking down
the stairs

Who's that walking down the stairs

Stomp,
stomp,

that's
my dad

'Stomp, stomp',
'Step, step, step' and
'Clatter bang crash'
along with the song to
develop rhythm and
pulse skills.

Step,
step,
step,

that's
my mum

Why not try
these patterns
on a drum once
you know the
song?

bang

Clatter

that's
my brother

crash,

23

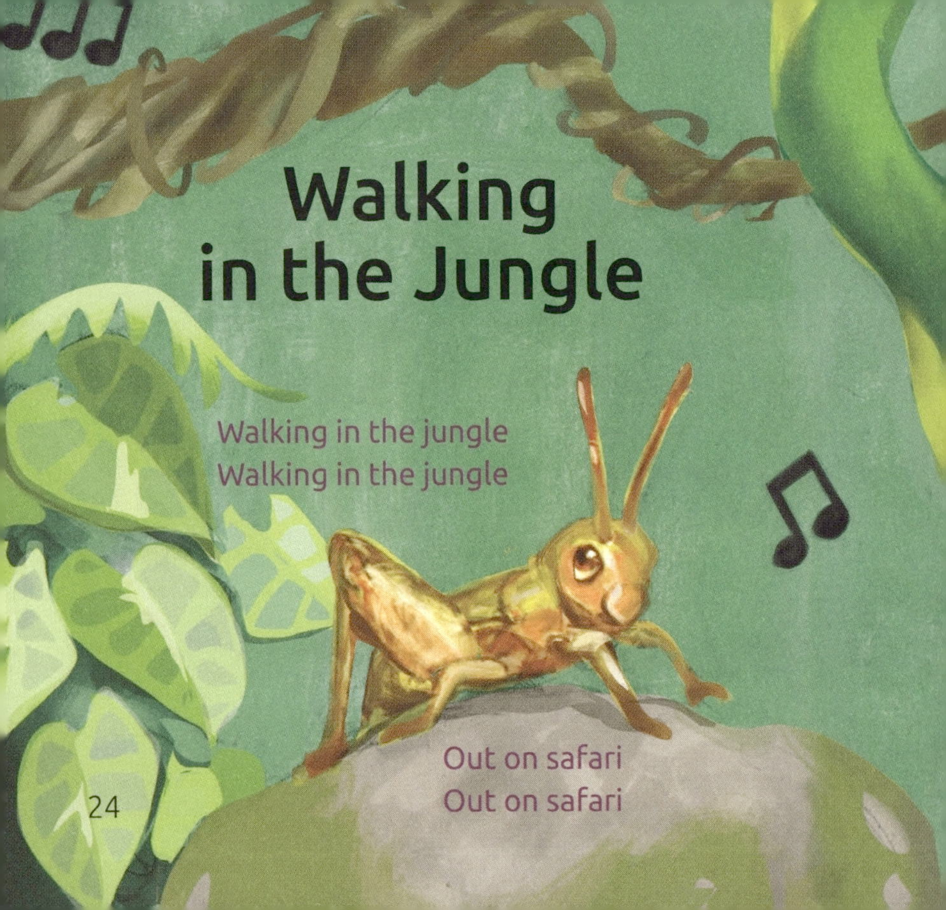
Walking
in the Jungle

Walking in the jungle
Walking in the jungle

Out on safari
Out on safari

24

Animals around us
Animals around us

What will we see in
the jungle today?

I can see an elephant,
what about you?

Say it loudly, say it
softly, repeating the
lines and moving
with the beat.

What can you see?
What can you see?

25

In the Jungle

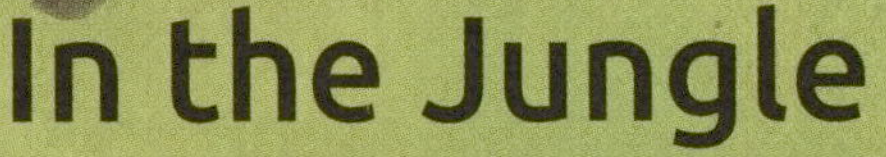

In the **jungle**, lots of trees live
Grass and flowers
growing up
tall

Monkeys climb ....
Snakes slide by ....

Crocodiles with open
mouths

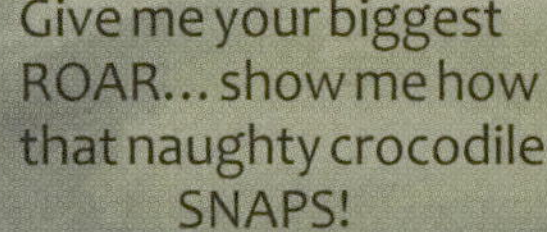

The roar of the tiger and 'sss' of the snake, the 'squawk' of the parrot are really useful for developing more complex speech sounds, as well as confidence in using the voice.

Cornelius the Octopus

Cornelius is Songo's special friend and loves to dance as well as sing.

Can you find some of Songo's other friends in this book?

Chorus
Co-co-Cornelius
......etc

Cornelius and his friends play all summer in the waves

A dolphin, a crab, a seahorse, and ....a shark

29

Good Morning
Dance along as you sing
'Good Morning'.
Good morning,
good morning,
how are you today?
30

I'm fine,
I'm fine
with a smile
upon my face

Smile and wave and take
turns – who can sing
'Good morning, good mor-
ning, how are you today'?

Who will answer 'I'm fine, I'm fine…'.

31

I Am Calling My Friend

I am calling my friend - *I am calling my friend*

Rachel is her name - *Rachel is her name*

I am calling my friend -

I am calling my friend

Rachel is her name -

Rachel is her name

32

I am here, I am here, I am here with all my friends
Rachel's here, Rachel's here,
Rachel's here with all her friends

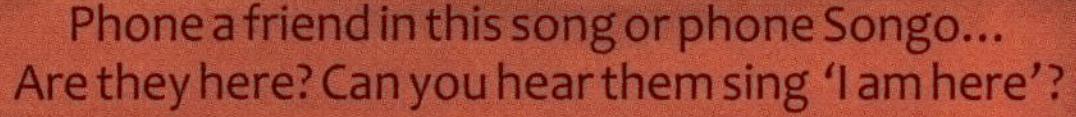

Phone a friend in this song or phone Songo…
Are they here? Can you hear them sing 'I am here'?

Like the song 'Hi There' developing the confidence
to sing a short solo in a song helps with personal
development and self-esteem.

33

We're Going to the Seaside

We're going to the seaside
We're going to the seaside

We're walking on the beach
We're walking on the beach

Jump in the water
Jump in the water

What do you see?
What do you see?

Dive into the water… what kind of things
will we find at the seaside?

Sand? Buckets and spades?
Crabs and seashells? Ice-cream?

35

The Sparkling Sea

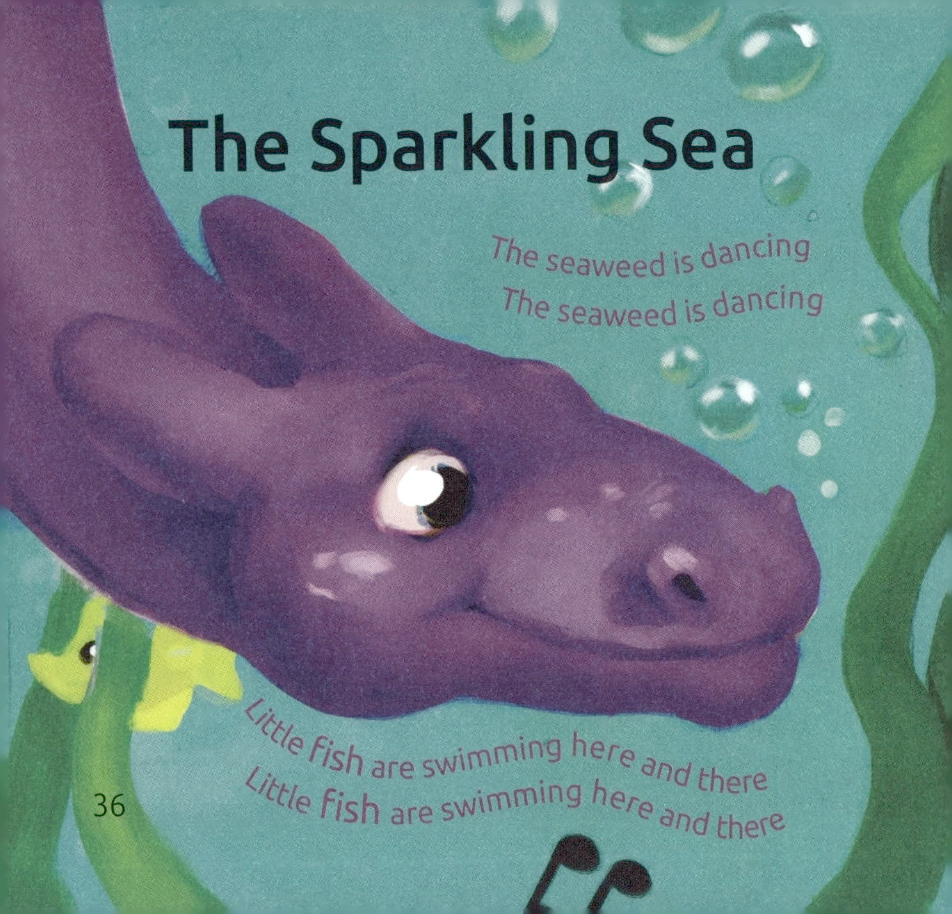

The seaweed is dancing
The seaweed is dancing

Little fish are swimming here and there
Little fish are swimming here and there

Under the green and sparkling sea
Under the green and sparkling sea
Enjoy the gentle rhythm of the song and dance like the seaweed.
Show me how the little fish swim around and the waves crash on the beach.
37

Henry's Tail

Down, down in the deep blue sea
Lived a fish and his name was Henry

Henry wasn't happy with the tail he had
It was short and brown he felt really sad

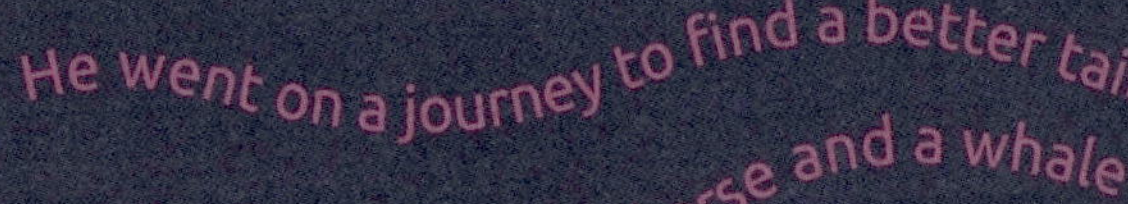

He went on a journey to find a better tail

 Met a shark and a mermaid, a seahorse and a whale

Can you remember the story of Henry's Tail
and tell it to Songo?

Clap the rhythm and if you have a drum you
can use that as well with the story.

39

I'm Going To...

I'm going to swim in the sea
I'm going to climb up a tree

I'm going to jump and I'm going to fly
Tomorrow I'll have fun, I'm going to try!

40

Tell Songo what you are going to do today.

Are you going to walk in the park? Are you going to play on the swings?... What are we doing right now?

Thinking and talking about the future as well as what's happening right now develops new language skills.

How Many Trees?

42

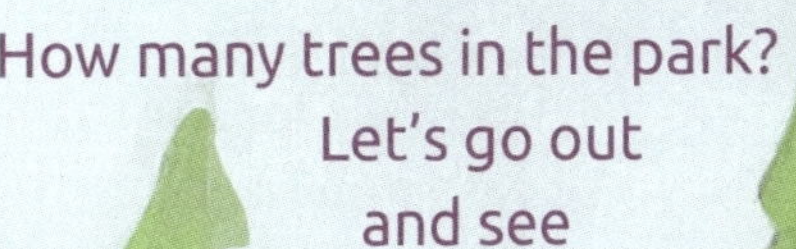

How many trees in the park?
Let's go out
and see

One, two,
One, two, three,
One, two, three, four, five

Show me how
you can count by
clapping, stamping
or tapping your
knees as you say the
numbers.

What else can
you count in the
park? 'How many
ducks on the
pond?'...

One, two,
One, two, three,
One, two, three, four, five

43

What Kind of Weather?

When the weather
is wet we go

splash,

splash,

splash

When the weather
is cold we go

brrrr...

Look out the window
What do you see?

What kind of coat do
you need today?

What kind of weather
do we have today?

What kind of coat, hat or
shoes do you need today?

Is it raining?
Is it sunny?

Do you need your
wellies, or a sunhat?

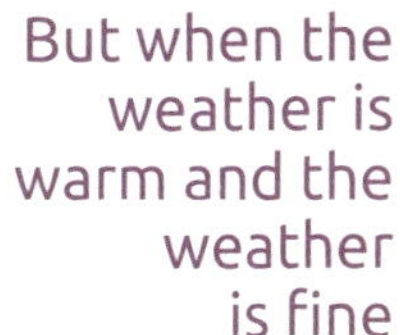

I've Lost My Dog

I've lost my dog
Where can he be?

Help Songo find
the lost dog.
Can you hear him?

Maybe he is hiding
under the chair or
behind the sofa?

If you see him
Can you bring him back to me?

✗2

46

Woof, woof, woof
That's my dog
Woof, woof, woof
That's my dog
Shout with me!
Where is my dog?
47

Acknowledgements

The songs in this book were composed for two Musiko Musika projects called i am here!! and WE ARE HERE!! This material was created by Musiko Musika with the support of funds awarded by Youth Music, registered charity no: 1075032. We are very grateful to all our funders: Youth Music, the Dr Edwards and Bishop Kings Fulham Charity and Hammersmith and Fulham Fast Track Funding for supporting those projects.

Lastly, thank you to the thousands of children we have worked with, their families and teachers, whose spirit and energy permeates this work, and to Victorina Press our publishers for their support in bringing this work to publication.

Credits

Songs and lyrics composed by:
Mauricio Venegas-Astorga and Rachel Pantin

Recorded at:
Tatu Music Studios London
Engineering by Mauricio Venegas-Astorga & Rachel Pantin
Mixed & Mastered by Mauricio Venegas-Astorga

Instrumentals: Mauricio Venegas-Astorga,
Rachel Pantin, Laura Venegas-Rojas
With guest: Diego Barrera (Cornelius the Octopus)
Vocals: Rachel Pantin, Laura Venegas-Rojas, Lizzie Smith,
Nikole Markova & the children of Musiko Musika's ECCO orchestra

Cover, graphic design and illustrations: Fiona Zechmeister

SONGO
SONGO
SONGO
SONGO
SONGO
SONGO